A·Boo·C

A Spooky Alphabet Story

By Pamela Jane
Illustrated by Maggie Smith

It's Halloween, so come with me.
We'll trick-or-treat from A to Z,
and stick a jewel on all we see!

To my own jewel, Annelise — P.J.

For Zach and Zoë — M.S.

Grosset & Dunlap · New York

Copyright © 1998 by Pamela Jane. Illustrations copyright © 1998 by Maggie Smith. All rights reserved. Published by Grosset & Dunlap, Inc., a member of Penguin Putnam Books for Young Readers, New York. GROSSET & DUNLAP is a trademark of Grosset & Dunlap, Inc. Published simultaneously in Canada. Printed in the U.S.A.
ISBN 0-448-41741-3 A B C D E F G H I J

A is for ANGEL with silvery wings.
B is for BRACELET. (It matches my rings!)

C is my COSTUME I made with my mother.

D is a DRAGON. (He's really my brother.)

Put a jewel on the object listed for each letter.

E is for EARRINGS that dance in the light.
F is for FORTUNE. (I'll tell yours tonight.)

G is for GHOST all wrapped in a sheet.

H is for HIGH HEELS that fall off my feet!

I is for ICE SKATER—
with skates laced up tight.

J is for JACK-O'-LANTERN, aglow in the night.

K is for KING
with a shiny gold crown.

L is for LIPSTICK to make up a clown.

M is for MONSTER; sometimes she's a pest.

N's her long NOSE. (It's my sister—you guessed!)

O is for **OWL**
who looks old and wise.

P is for PILGRIM.
It's Jenny—surprise!

R is for ROBOT.
(This one makes me laugh!)

S is for SKELETON.
(This one's not too scary.)

T is for TREASURE
the two pirates carry.

U is for UNICORN
who prances and leaps.

V is a VAMPIRE.
(He gives me the creeps!)

W is for WITCH.
(Do you think she can fly?)

Y is for YELLOW; the moon high and clear.

Z is ZOOM home! (No jewel needed here.)